Seasons of Change

I0675636

Sim Johnson

Published by Richter Publishing LLC
www.richterpublishing.com

Book Cover Design: Richter Publishing LLC

Editor: Maurice Jovan Billington & Monica San Nicolas

ISBN: 978-1-945812-71-2

DISCLAIMER

This book is designed for entertainment purposes only. This information is provided and sold with the knowledge that the publisher and author do not offer any legal or medical advice. It is a work of fiction. In the case of a need for any such expertise consult with the appropriate professional. This book does not contain all information available on the subject. This book has not been created to be specific to any individual people or organization's situation or needs. Reasonable efforts have been made to make this book as accurate as possible. However, there may be typographical and or content errors. Therefore, this book should serve only as a general guide. This book contains information that might be dated or erroneous and is intended only to entertain. The author and publisher shall have no liability or responsibility to any person or entity regarding any loss or damage incurred, or alleged to have incurred, directly or indirectly, by the information contained in this book or as a result of anyone acting or failing to act upon the information in this book. You hereby agree never to sue and to hold the author and publisher harmless from any and all claims arising out of the information contained in this book. You hereby agree to be bound by this disclaimer, covenant not to sue and release. All characters appearing in this work are fictitious. Any resemblance to other real persons, living or dead, is purely coincidental. The opinions and stories in this book are the views of the authors and not those of the publisher.

CONTENTS

PROLOGUE

FOR EVERY TIME A SEASON

My name is Sara. I would tell you my last name but the town I live in is so small no one ever uses them. You either know everyone's first name or you're not from here. We like it that way. I know my parents did before they were suddenly gone, vanished as if the world blinked and when it reopened its eyes it forgot where it put them.

My grandmother, Nova, never attempted to explain where they went. She just said, "One day,

Sunflower…" She called me her little sunflower. "One day," she would say, "They will return."

I had no choice but to believe her, even though when I looked into my grandfather's eyes, I saw only sadness. But my grandmother had never lied to me before, so I had no choice to believe her, even though my grandfather's eyes never lied either.

My grandfather was a great man. I understand fully why my grandmother fell in love with him beneath a blue sky, as she would often reminisce. She could recall that day as if she were experiencing it while telling it.

"The sky was a translucent blue," she'd say. "So blue it was as if you looked deep enough into it, you became a part of it, disappearing into its brilliance. And the wind," she'd continue, "The wind blew just enough to let you know it was there without disturbing any ot the landscape that surrounded you."

I always asked her to tell me more. And she

would. She was riding her favorite horse, Anemos, her parents, my great grandparents raised horses then sold them, but Anemos was hers. It was when she was riding on this particular blue sky day, further than she had before, that she saw Irvin Wheeler, only twenty at the time. Irvin was standing beneath a tree with branches so sprawling, they acted as an umbrella for both of them to be beneath.

My grandfather, my grandmother says, was looking up at the tree, so transfixed that he did not notice she was there until Anemos announced it for her.

He turned to her, looking up to her atop the horse even though he was quite tall himself.

"Beautiful," he said. And she smiled... not knowing whether he was talking about her, Anemos, or the tree.

It is her favorite memory.

I have my own favorite memory of my

grandparents.

My grandparents were scientists. They were not the type of scientists confined by the four walls of a laboratory or the boredom of numbers. My grandparents were environmental scientists. The world was their lab. The beauty of a breeze was the equations they studied to make sense of what sustained us and more importantly what could harm us. Not that they thought the earth was vindictive… but protective… and if man did not protect nature, nature at some point would protect itself.

This was not popular science. Science that restricts the behavior of man's worst inclinations never is. My grandparents were however unconcerned with popular and more focused on important. This isn't to say that they were doom and gloom. No. My grandparents held inside them the joy of a hummingbird with a heart that beats fast and fierce in the sole pursuit of the sweetest nectar from the most beautiful of flowers.

Which brings me back to my most favorite memory with them.

It was my birthday. I had just turned thirteen. It was just the three of us in an open field beneath an equally beautiful blue sky as the first day they met.

My grandmother had prepared my favorite meal. Bologna and cheese sandwiches with peanut butter instead of mayonnaise. There was pink lemonade and red balloons.

We talked and joked and laughed and my grandfather pointed out the activity and reasons why of every insect that crashed my private party. It was the perfect afternoon.

I remember walking back to our farmhouse holding the one red balloon in my hand that had not succumbed to the heat. As we walked closer and closer to our home I remember looking up at the sky and the sun. I remember the sun being so bright but almost as if a present to me, it shone away from my eyes so that I could admire its brilliance. I wanted to give it a present in return. So, I released the balloon.

I watched as the balloon slowly floated upwards almost reticent to leave me but happy to be free. I watched and watched and watched as it got higher and higher and higher. It was easy to see because the sky was so blue and it was so red. So bright red. The sun at some point turned its attention to the color competing with its own and allowed me to see it just a little bit longer.

It felt like I watched that balloon ascend up to the sky for an hour. It felt like it was carrying me up and away with it as it did.

That was when I was thirteen. That was when my grandparents were still alive. That was when the place and the world in which I lived wrapped its arms around me as if substituting for the loss of my parents.

Things change. Everything changes. Sometimes it is for the better good and sometimes it is because of the greater evil. But everything, everything changes eventually. A time for every season.

Now I am 30. I still live in the same town. I still

live in the same house. But the landscape has changed. And not for the better good.

The weather is angry. The sky is red. And they were warned. They all were. But you don't listen when the sky is blue. You don't change when you don't have to. You only start to wonder what is wrong when you release a red balloon into the sky and you can't see it three seconds later because the clouds are on fire and red completely surrounds you.

But by then... when you have angered what sustains you... when you have taken for granted what protected you... when you have not even an apology to give because you don't know what you did wrong... It's too late.

Unless someone visits you that knew it was coming.

CHAPTER 1

2050

(FLASH FORWARD)

A rope falls from the top of an opening about 100 feet down into what looks like the middle of woods... a forest... it is difficult to tell because of the almost pitch black darkness. In fact, the only light emanates from the intertwined coils of the rope that are illuminated from within.

A second rope descends down beside it, adding even more light to what now might be a cave. What seemed like hundreds of branches now appear to be perhaps stalactites.

And then there was light.

Two bodies descend down the ropes, one but seconds apart from the other. The source of added light coming from their Hazmat-like suits that are completed illuminated, as if constructed of the same material of the rope. Additional light focused into a beam, and more translucent than the white of the suit is supplied atop the headgear both invaders don.

The environment they have entered is now apparent. They appear to be beneath the earth, in a cavernous area that allows them to move freely. What appeared to be tree limbs are actually the roots of trees… long, thick, majestic and surrounding them, beyond them, above them and beside them.

Both explorers have holsters around their waist both with some sort of gun-like weapon at the ready.

"It's beautiful," a female voice intones as she

looks around at the life sustaining roots and the water that cascades down them like drops of rain then down to their feet.

She is young, 24, maybe 25. She is also beautiful. Caramel complexed, big, brown, expressive eyes and straight black hair that can be seen through the clear face shield of the protective helmet she wears.

"Don't be afraid," an older male voice says. She turns to him, looking at him through his face shield. He is, like her, very young, 26, Caucasian, brown haired, blue eyed and handsome.

The female smiles as she responds. "I was going to tell you that."

Now the male smiles back. "Sorry. Comes with the job… you know… protect and serve."

"Well, I promise to protect you," she begins. "But if we make it through this, I will be expecting you to serve that dinner you promised me."

"When did I promise you a dinner?"

"Just now," she playfully responds.

A sound interrupts them. Both turn and look in the same direction pouring light down the long and mysterious way in front of them.

"What's that?" the male voice asks.

"It's them."

"Is it OK to be afraid now," he responds.

"Sure," she says as she slowly pulls out the weapon at her side and holds it in front of her.

"I'll be brave for the both of us."

CHAPTER 2

A Winterless Snow

The year was 2045. That was the year the people of my town first began to take notice of the change in the weather. Like any Northern town seasonal change was expected. But change within that change became something altogether different.

I was a nurse at Bolt General Hospital. Growing up, I never dreamed nor thought about being in the medical field. As a matter of fact, the sight of blood, even the tiniest amount made me lightheaded. But when my grandparents both fell ill that all changed.

I watched as the doctors struggled to diagnose their illness, and worse, ignored my grandparent's pleas to be let go to find the help they knew was out there.

You see, my grandparents were quarantined, though not at first, after their mysterious ailment began to worsen. It started with their breathing. Both, almost simultaneously, became short of breath, but the doctors attributed it to their age and activity that never slowed. By the time they began losing color in their skin at a rate so alarming, they were kept away from every other patient in the hospital.

The doctors never figured out what had befallen them. One day, as quickly as they had gotten sick, and again, simultaneously, they passed gently into the night.

Years later, at a considerable expense, paid for by the sale of the few remaining horses my grandparents owned, I was a nurse.

I may have been the first to notice something was wrong.

I remember walking down the corridors of the hospital and noticing the number of elderly people there. Now, elderly patients are not a red flag at a hospital, nor is the reason most where there, heat stroke. But it was December. And any given December the average temperature was in the 40s. I had already been disappointed by the uncharacteristic lack of snow, but when the temperature rose that day to 101 degrees… I then became worried.

I wasn't the only one. The entire town of Tailsview, population four thousand, began asking questions not only of Jim Jergins, or JJ, as we called our local weatherman, but of Deputy Pete.

Deputy Pete, no last name used as it was deemed entirely too formal of a town our size, was a kind soul of about 26 years of age. He was handsome in a throwback sort of way, almost like a cowboy from the 1800s. His hat, and the manner in which he wore it all the time, added to his young man born in the wrong century charm.

The complaints in the beginning were not only not alarming, but to be expected. "Hey JJ, when is the snow coming?" was a common one. "Why is it so hot?" quickly followed with the same repetition.

That was October. By November, when the first flakes of snow had yet to fall, the questions became more direct. "Are we experiencing Global Warming? That's actually a thing?" And then we found ourselves in December.

In December, the questions became more statements than queries. "It has to be terrorists," or, spoken with very little conviction, "I'm sure there's nothing to worry about." Mostly though the primary statement was, "Damn the big cities." You see, we lived simply, we lived clean, and if there was some problem with the ozone, it wasn't because private jets were flying in and out of our non-existent airport.

Deputy Pete handled the constant barrage of rants with his characteristic good nature. He was not one to dismiss a concern. But as he watched good townspeople, townspeople he had taken an oath to protect, fall ill because of the heat, he started having questions of his own. The problem was, no one seemed to have the answers.

Information from what we often jokingly referred to as, 'The outside world,' which was any part of the world not Tailsview, was non-existent. It was understandable. They weren't affected. There was no news reports of unseasonable weather, nor masses of people affected by heat stroke. There were certainly no reports of people passing as my grandparents had. There was just us. Tailsview.

Deputy Pete wisely decided to start holding weekly town meetings as the temperature remained at 101 for the third week in a row. Even if he were unable to answer the townspeople's concerns, it would at least guarantee he could walk down the streets for at least ten minutes without being stopped.

The weekly meetings were not just Q&A sessions. Supplies, mostly donated, would be given out to those that needed them. These supplies included, fans, bottles of water and in some cases even air conditioning units for those that had failed under the stress of constant operation.

It was about the third week that we were joined by two people from the "Outside World".

"Hello…" we hear, before the door to the town church, where our meetings were held, can close.

In steps the Winderbergs. Sam Winderberg looks to be about 70 years of age, while his wife Leslie looks not too much younger. Both are white haired, pale skinned with piercing blue eyes that can be seen from across the church as if they were standing right before you.

"I hope we didn't interrupt," Mr. Winderberg continues.

Deputy Pete is the first to respond. "No. You didn't."

"Good," Mr. Winderberg responds.

"Can I help you?" Deputy Pete asks.

An odd smile draws across Mrs. Winderberg's face, and it makes her seems decades younger.

"No," Mr. Winderberg responds. We're here to help you."

CHAPTER 3

The Calm Before

Sam and Leslie invite us in, almost as if expecting both Deputy Pete and me. How could they not at the very least expect the sheriff after such an ominous introduction. Indeed, as soon as they left the church, almost immediately after uttering their intentions, Deputy Pete followed, and I followed him.

They led us to a small wooden house on the

outskirts of town that if you had asked me earlier, I would have sworn to you had been abandoned for years. But as we pulled up in the Sheriff's police car, we were both shocked to see a dwelling that looked as if it had never been vacant. In fact, it looked as if it belonged in another town.

The unseasonably hot weather had scorched every yard dry. But the Winderberg's was a vibrant green, replete with a towering oak that must have taken a century to grow but I promise you, on the few occasions I had to pass this property, I had never seen.

We step in and are no less surprised to see a home full of plants and flowers so colorful and abundant it's as if we have stepped into a greenhouse.

"How beautiful," I say, "Simply beautiful."

"Why thank you," Mrs. Winderberg says. "I wish I could take credit, but my husband has the green thumb."

"But how…" I begin when Deputy Pete gently nudges me by the side, which does not go unnoticed by Mr. Winderberg.

"It's OK," Mr. Winderberg states. "Of course you have questions. I expect by the end of this visit you will have many more."

"Well, now that you mention it," Deputy Pete intones, "I was sort of wondering what you meant back at the church. How are you going to help us? And with what?"

"Please, sit down," Mr. Winderberg says, and we do. It is then I begin to notice other things about that seem, well, odd. Like how warm the house is, again, like a hothouse, but how neither of the Winderberg's are sweating. The heat alone should have beads of water upon their foreheads like Deputy Pete and me, but nothing. The fact that they are both wearing long sleeves ensures that it should.

I feel compelled to ask, but I remember the

nudge by Pete. And he is sitting close enough beside me to nudge me again, so I remain quiet.

Mr. Winderberg pulls four crystals from his pocket and extends them toward us.

"What are those?" I ask.

"These..." Mr. Winderberg begins, "Are the answers to your questions.

"They look like crystals." Pete states and Mr. Winderberg nods in agreement.

"That's exactly what they are. Four," he says. "Each one representing the four seasons. Winter, spring, summer and fall."

Deputy Pete smiles. "Yes," he says. "I'm familiar with the seasons. But how are four crystals going to help us here in Tailsview?

A serious look washes over Mr. Winderberg's face. He pulls the crystals back to him as he leans forward to speak. Both Pete and I instinctively lean in as if we know something is coming. Something we have been waiting for.

"Change," Mr. Winderberg says.

"Change?" I respond ahead of Deputy Pete.

"Change, Sunflower," he says, and I'm immediately struck silent by the fact that he knows the name my grandmother used to call me.

"How..." I try to get out... But he interrupts me to continue his train of thought.

"Change is coming to Tailsview... Just like the seasons change. And if you are going to survive... The change of seasons is your only hope."

CHAPTER 4

The Storm

We are back in the police cruiser. Both of us are silent. Both of us look ahead as we travel down the road, only this time back to Tailsview proper. And both of us know no more than what we did before we arrived at the Winderbergs.

The only difference is that I now hold four crystals in my hand. Deputy Pete glances down, momentarily taking his eyes from the road at my tightly closed fist.

"Maybe you can make a necklace out of them one day." He jokes. It's kinda funny, so I somewhat laugh.

"You're not funny," I lie. And he knows it, because, well, I'm laughing. "What was that?" I continue.

"What was what?" he replies.

"You know."

"Yeah… I do," he acknowledges. "I don't know, Sunflower…" I interrupt him.

"Don't…"

"Don't what?" he smiles.

"Don't you dare call me, Sunflower," I say. "Only my grandmother ever called me that."

"Then how did he..." I interrupt him again knowing what the question is.

"I don't know how he knew. I answer. "Maybe he didn't. Maybe it was just a..."

"Just a what?" Pete asks because I have stopped mid-sentence.

I have stopped because I am staring out into the distance through the windshield of the car, and I am unsure of what I am seeing.

The sky is red. That is an anomaly that I am now used to. But as I look out into the horizon, it seems as if the road we are on, a road with nothing on either side but dust that, too, seems red in color, as if ash is presently burning. It seems as if the road is directing us straight into an inferno.

If you're young enough to remember the California wildfires when there was a California before the fires burned it all away, then you'd know what I mean. There's archival footage of residents fleeing their towns at night, the roads and sky lit up by fire on either side. Well, it is day, but darkness lies ahead. Darkness that appears lit by slowly growing red.

Deputy Pete refocuses his attention on the front of the road and now his eyes go wide.

"What in the …"

He doesn't need to say the last word. It looks as if we are driving toward it.

"I'm turning around he says."

"No. You're not." I respond.

"Why not?"

He doesn't know that I have already looked behind us, but my silence compels him to and when he does, he then understands.

"Oh." He says.

"Look!" I shout. Drawing his attention back to the road ahead, but more specifically the sky that is raining. Raining fire. Fire all around us.

"What do we do?" he asks as if I know any more than him.

"Drive." I say. "Drive really fast!"

"I think you're right!" Deputy Pete then presses his foot down on the gas and with no other choice we are now speeding down the road away from the fire into the furnace.

As the skies open with a hellish glow, as embers of ash float in the air like particles of snow, visibility becomes greatly diminished. Deputy Pete turns on the emergency lights of his patrol car and now swaths of blue intermittently slice through the red like sword.

Pete looks over at me. He can see what he perceives is panic on my face. But he's wrong. It's actually concern.

"Don't worry. I'm not going to let anything happen to us." He tries to reassure. He doesn't.

"What about the town?" I say. "You can't protect us all." And then he understands the look on my face as he slowly turns back to the road.

The next thing I know we are going faster as if Pete has put his foot through the floor where the gas pedal is. Flames whip by us as ash swirls around us and I realize I can no longer see the road ahead. And I know Pete cannot either.

"My god..." Pete whispers. "How did the

weather change so fast?"

And then I remember Mr. Winderberg's words. They seemed odd at the time but now I think I understand. 'Change,' he said. 'Change of seasons is your only hope.'

I look down at my tightly clenched fist. I slowly open my fingers and stare at the four crystals within. I notice that there is now a slight color variation in each. This is something I had not noticed before because it had not been there. Was it the pressure of my grasp? Was it the sweat from my grip? Or was it the heat from outside slowly creeping inside? Or... Or was it a sign?

I focus on the crystal glowing blue. It is a cool blue. Cool like a winter's morning. Winter. Season. A change of seasons is our only hope.

I go to roll down the window and Deputy Pete quickly grabs my hand to stop me.

"What are you doing? You'll let the fire inside?"

"It already is," I tell him.

"Then what are you doing?"

"Trust me," I respond. And the look in his eyes, his silence, answers that he does.

I press the button, lowering the window halfway. I raise the blue crystal in my hand having put aside the other three. It seems to glow bluer the closer it gets to the window.

"What are you doing?" Pete asks.

"Changing the season." And I release the crystal out of my hand and into the fire.

CHAPTER 5

The Quickening Frost

We slowly pull up to the town... We have to drive slowly because the streets are full of the townspeople. Everyone is outside. Everyone.

I look over to Deputy Pete. He is speechless. I don't blame him. With the oppressive heat, if you were to see four people outside, you were either lucky or seeing double. But now, every hidden face is out, and they are all doing the exact same thing. Looking up to the sky at the falling snow. That's right, I said snow.

"It's beautiful," Deputy Pete says softly.

"I know," I respond. He turns to me and smiles. I love his smile. It makes his eyes shine. What's even cuter is that he is wholly unaware of both those facts.

"You did this," he says. I smile. Not because I'm taking the credit he is giving me, but because he is still smiling.

We drive further into the town until we reach the church where familiar faces await us on the stairs. From the look on their faces, it is as if they somehow know that we are somehow responsible.

Once inside the church the questions come

faster than can be answered but we both try.

No, we don't know how the weather changed, but yes, It has something to do with Mr. and Mrs. Winderberg. And no... We still have no idea who they actually are, what they want and how long this strange winter will last.

The possibility that if they brought the cold perhaps they are responsible for the intolerable heat before it is implied enough that Deputy Pete must address it.

"Listen," he starts. "I wish I could tell you that the Winderbergs are good people. They certainly seem so. But as the law you don't want to hear what I think you want to hear what I know. And I simply don't know enough."

"But it's your job to know, right?" Tarber Zane asks.

Tarber is always asking. That's what he's known for in a town where everyone is known for something. Now there is nothing inherently wrong with asking questions, no, not at all. It's the manner in which he asks, almost as if he knows the answer but is testing you to see if you know it as well. Tarber doesn't asking a question seeking an answer, he wants validation of what he already believes.

"I mean, after losing the Sheriff and every other deputy to the Dry," he continues. "You're for better or for worse the only law we have."

"And?" Deputy Pete responds.

"And if you don't know what's going on," Tarber answers back. "Then maybe someone else should be."

"You can't put this on Pete," I interject. "He's been affected more than just about anyone."

"You lost your grandparents," he shoots back.

"We don't know that their illness had anything to do with the changes in the weather.

"We don't?" he asks in that exact same manner in which I previously described. How many people got sick as the weather got weird and died in the exact same manner. Sure, the doctors in the city said it was some unknown virus. Well, it's still unknown. And there are still people dying.

"Including Deputy Pete's best friend, as you just pointed out." I snap back. "So, what's your point?"

"My point is somebody has to know something. Things like this don't just happen. And when they do, it's usually the people in charge of things that know why. You two leave and when you come back you've brought cold with you. Cold that probably saved the lives of everyone in this town."

"Including yours." Deputy Pete adds.

"Yeah. Including me. So why don't you tell me who I should thank."

There's silence as both Deputy Pete and I look at each other. Then, Tarber looks straight at me.

"Should I thank you, Sara?" he asks. "Did you save the town?"

"She may have saved the world." One of the townspeople says as she steps over and initializes the feature on her phone that brings up the video image of what she is watching which enables everyone around to see. "Look at this." She says. And we do.

What we see is a news report showing scenes all over the world, a world once inexplicably burning now slowly being covered by a soft blanket of snow. Even in regions of summer, there was snow.

Now everyone turns and looks at Deputy Pete and I. Waiting for an answer. That is, until we see a slow change in the images on the floating screen.

The snow in every city, every region, every land, everywhere begins to stop. And the powder white skies give way to an oppressive hue of red, which reminds us how close the heat is to fire.

I turn to the doors of the church and slowly walk toward them and once there, I open them and look out and up to the burning sky.

"I didn't save anything," I whisper.

Deputy Pete steps up beside me and looks out as well. We are soon joined by the entire group.

"Well, that didn't last long," I hear someone say behind me. And then... out of nowhere, literally we all hear a sound coming from down the road.

Through the haze of heat, it is difficult to see the source of the sound but as it gets louder and louder it reveals itself. A caravan of trucks, box trucks, rather large box trucks slowly roll down Main Street, kicking up a considerable amount of dust in their wake.

In between the box trucks are trailer trucks loaded with materials we cannot determine but it looks like enough material to build a city.

The vehicles are all headed in the direction of the Winderberg's home.

"Looks like we're going back to the Winderberg's," Deputy Pete says. And I agree.

CHAPTER 6

A Frozen Future

By the time Deputy Pete and I arrive back to the Winderbergs, the "visitors", as Deputy Pete termed them on the car ride, have already exited their vehicles and begun to unload the equipment and items we are still not sure of.

The Winderbergs stand on the steps of their home observing. They smile as we exit the car and walk over to them.

It almost seems as if they expected us, again.

"Planning on adding to the house?" Deputy Pete asks, somewhat in jest.

"Well," Mr. Winderberg begins, "We actually are planning on some additions. We'd love to file the proper permits but I'm not sure there will be time."

"Time...?" I inquire. "Time for what?"

Before either of the Winderbergs can answer, a car pulls up beside Deputy Pete's. I turn and look and know immediately who the car belongs to. Tarber. Though he is not alone.

I also know the person exiting the car from the passenger side door. She is smiling but I am not. Her name is Agnes Wroder, and in a town as I said, where everybody is known for something, Agnes is known for wanting to know everything. Now that isn't necessarily a bad thing, but it is a dangerous thing when you only seek knowledge to know how to go counter to it.

Agnes has probably spent the better part of her 40 plus years being a contrarian. This makes Tarber her perfect pupil. Despite the age difference they are definitely of like mind with Agnes pulling the strings of conspiracy.

"Sara…" Agnes smiles as she walks up to both Deputy Pete and me. I nod hello with only a half-smile. "Deputy Pete," she says as she looks over at him.

"Agnes, good morning." He responds.

"Is it morning still?" she asks. "With this heat the way it is I lose track of time. Though we did get a bit of respite. Didn't we." She adds. She then looks over to the Winderbergs and smiles that very same smile. "My friend Tarber tells me we may have you to thank for that," she says to them. The Winderbergs just stand there and smile. "I'm Agnes. Agnes Wroder," she says, finally introducing herself as Tarber steps up and stands beside her.

"If I'd have known we were going to have so many visitors I would have made coffee," Mrs. Winderberg states. "Why don't you all come inside."

And so we do. And we find ourselves, the four of us from town, staring at the two people that have yet to tell us where they are from.

But this is what they do tell us, and you too may find it difficult to believe.

"The world is going to freeze." Those are the six words uttered by Mrs. Winderberg that commands our attention until they are finished.

She continues by informing us that our world was on the precipice of a second Ice Age. That it was inevitable and unstoppable. The unbearable heat we were now experiencing was due to man's constant denial of global warming and the effects it could have on us all... Nature, she explained, was the most powerful force on Earth. The ultimate sustainer of life itself. Without the balance of nature maintained, then life would become chaos until it ultimately extinguished.

She told of how the earth's fever is about to break and when it does nature will plunge it into a deep freeze to eliminate whatever virus caused the fever.

She said "we" were the virus. She said unlike certain organisms that would reanimate during the thaw and repopulate, humans would not be amongst those. We would not survive. Simply put... Nature was going to protect itself against those that would not protect it.

"There has to be something that we can do," I say. That is when Mr. Winderberg begins.

"Fortunately," he says, "There are things that were put in place to protect both nature and humans. A species that was a part of both. A species that understood that though nature could exist without mankind it was not meant to. That people served an absolute purpose on this planet beyond what even we understood.

I ask if they are that species of being, but he would not answer. He would only smile.

He elaborated by explaining that those meant to protect both nature and us would accelerate the inevitable freeze with just our town. That we would be used as a sort of example for the rest of the world to observe and that the choices we made would either convince them to do the same or die when the freeze became worldwide.

"Why us?" Deputy Pete asks what we all had to be thinking as we sat there and listened. Then adding, "We didn't ask for this."

He told us that it didn't matter whether we asked to be chosen or not. That we were all chosen the moment we were born, and one person's failure was everyone's failure. That is how connected the universe is. And it was up to us to choose now, we as a people had failed so bad that the choice was going to be made for us.

There was more... a lot more... but first the four

of us had to get some air.

CHAPTER 7

When All Do Not Believe

This was not going to be a nice conversation. I knew that from the look on Agnes Wroder's face through most of the conversation, but I also knew that because I knew Agnes Wroder. Even standing before God, she would still ask him to make a bush burn before she would believe.

That's why the Tarber is the perfect lapdog for her. Young, though a year older than myself, but never having accomplished anything other than annoying everyone in town with his constant conspiracy theories and wild beliefs.

"I'm not going back in there," is the first thing she states. "And I hope you aren't dumb enough to either, though somehow..."

"Somehow what?" I interrupt. And she can gather from the tone in my voice and the look in my eyes that perhaps, just perhaps, she shouldn't continue. So, she wisely changes course of conversation.

"Clearly these people are insane," she throws out. "Insane. Now I can't tell you what they're after but at some point, it will lead to money as it always does. People trying to profit off of plight. I've seen it a thousand times."

Have you seen weather like this before? Have you seen the miracle of snow that you just witnessed, before…"

"Ha. Miracle," she laughs. "An anomaly."

"Aren't you the least curious about whether they are right or not?" I look over to Tarber. "I know you must be. Their story is the stuff you dream of."

"No… I think Ms. Wroder is right. Even for me this sounds out there."

I motion to the constant motion of the workers unloading materials around us.

"And what about them? What about what they are doing? Aren't you the least bit curious?"

"I think the Deputy should be," Agnes snaps back. "But as for me, I've seen and heard enough. Enjoy your snake oil."

Agnes turns and begins toward the car with Tarber just a few feet behind her. I look over to the mysterious workers and notice that none of them have paid or are paying any attention to us. It's as if we do not exist to them. Or... They do not exist to us.

I look back over to Agnes and just as she is reaching for the handle of the car door something odd happens.

Shrubs at the far end of the landscape of the home burst into flames. The fire is immediately intense, requiring no time to build. And oddly... very oddly... there is no smoke. Only fire. A fire that reaches almost impossibly high into the air.

Remember what I said about Agnes and God. I'm not telling you God had anything to do with it. More than likely the shrubs burst into flames because of the searing heat. But Agnes lowers her hand from the car door and turns back to me.

"I'll meet you back inside," I say. Then I smile,

turn around and walk back into the home.

CHAPTER 8

Shelter from the Sky

We are back in the home of the Winderbergs. All of us, including Agnes. The expression of doubt, mistrust and condescension remains on her face.

As Mr. Winderberg is about to begin again, the noise from the workers outside intensifies. I glance out the window and see that large sheets of some unknown material are now being removed from the trucks. The sheets are so wide that a crane attached to the back of one of the trucks is used to off load them. I wonder what they are for. I don't have to wonder long.

Mr. Winderberg explains that what the worker bees, as he calls them, are doing is removing materials that will save us. Save us from the freezing sky.

"Domes," he says.

"Domes?" I respond.

"Yes." He answers back. "If you are to survive... if the world is to survive, then the people Tailsview must build domes to protect yourselves from the Icing."

"Domes," I say again. Not because I don't understand him, but like Agnes, I am having trouble believing.

"Sunflower..." Mr. Winderberg says softly, again referring to me by a nickname he should not know. "It is you that will lead them."

"Why me?" I rightfully ask.

"You are the chosen one." Mrs. Winderberg answers.

"Chosen by who?" Deputy Pete asks. It is Mr. Winderberg that answers the question. Well, sort of.

"By those who do the choosing."

Agnes stands. "I've heard enough," she says. "The fact is there is no coming frost... or icing as you call it. There is no global warming. This is just going to be an unseasonably hot Summer and then it's going to go away."

I stand and I turn directly to Agnes.

"People are dying!" I say. "This is not unseasonably hot, it's deadly. And while you may not care about anyone but yourself, I took an oath... an oath to protect the sick and dying, make them better to the best of my capabilities and if what these people are saying is true then that's what I'm going to do."

"That..." Mrs. Winderberg begins, "Is why you were chosen."

"Well, I didn't choose her, and no one leads me but myself. And I will not help build any domes and I certainly won't be staying inside one."

"Then you'll die," Mr. Winderberg says flatly. Anyone in Tailsview outside of the domes when the icing arrives will eventually die.

"I'll take my chances," she states. Then she turns to me. "You're not going to convince me to go into a cage and lock myself in while total strangers run around our town taking and doing whatever they please. And that's exactly what's going to happen.

"Remember the pandemic of 2020?" Tarber says, now chiming in. "The whole world went into lockdown and businesses were lost and lives were ruined. Some still say a lockdown wasn't necessary and just because it's a little hot outside I don't think one is now.

"A little hot..." Deputy Pete intones. "The sky is on fire."

"I don't care if the sky is falling," Agnes adds. "I'm not going into a dome."

With that, both she and Tarber excuse themselves and leave. No one attempts to stop them. And once they are gone, the Winderbergs detail the incredible task before the town.

Mr. Winderberg explained that the "worker bees" still currently unloading materials would demonstrate the process by which the domes would be built and then would leave to bring the town as much materials as they would need to replicate the process. And it would be a lot.

This wasn't going to be the building of one dome, so to speak; it was going to be the construction of a sea full.

Both Deputy Pete and I listened intently as we were told enough domes would need to be constructed to provide shelter for the entire population of the town.

"But what if there are those like Agnes that resist?" Deputy Pete asked. "And there will be." He added.

Mrs. Winderberg told us that she was sure Deputy Pete was correct. That there would be those that would not only not participate in the "sheltering", as she termed it, but would laugh at those that did. And even more ominously, she foretold of those that would attempt to prevent us from achieving our goal.

"There are those…" she began, "That do not want people to believe what they themselves cannot. Faith frightens them. And when people are scared, they will do anything within their powers to eliminate the fear."

Deputy Pete and I both remained silent. Both of us not altogether certain we even believed them, but if we were to, to now grasp townspeople might be turned against townspeople… What would we be signing up for?

"This sounds like an impossible undertaking." I say.

"It is," Mr. Winderberg replies.

"Then why should we try?" I ask.

"Because trying," Mr. Winderberg begins, "Is the

only way the impossible becomes possible."

"How long before this… this 'icing', as you call it?" Deputy Pete inquires.

We are told that in the coming weeks the intensifying heat will begin a reverse. A slow reverse. Almost imperceptible. A degree a week. This would give us the time we would need to begin, but then we are told the temperature of the weather would then drop a degree a day… and if we were not near completion by then, we might never reach it.

"A degree a day," I say. And it is confirmed by both the Winderbergs. "That might give us a month… maybe two depending on what the temperature is when it begins to fall that rapidly."

"Time…" Mr. Winderberg begins, "Is always the enemy of man. Especially when they fail to recognize it first starts out as their friend."

"So, what do you suggest?" Deputy Pete asks.

"I suggest we begin."

CHAPTER 9

The Old World

No one respects the elderly anymore. Perhaps it has been that way forever, but I can only remember as far back as my grandparents.

I remember the tree they met beneath as my mother rode Anemos. It still stands, majestic, magnificent, untouched by time which seems impossible because nature changes everything.

How can it not? Like the Earth that never stops spinning nature never ceases its progression. The rains come, and they stop but inevitably come again. Flowers bloom, they die, but other flowers spring forth from the same place. Seasons change... well, at least they did in the old world.

The next few months after that fateful meeting with the Winderbergs, even as Agnes remained steadfast in her denial of the coming frost, the people of Tailsview joined forces with the worker bees as the Winderbergs referred to them to begin the construction of the domes.

This is not to say the decision to trust in the stranger's pronouncement of impending doom was easy or instantaneously unanimous. It was not.

The church was the location for many meetings where words that should never be uttered in a house of God were spoken. I mean, imagine attempting to build a bridge to the new world when so many don't want to leave the old. It has always been this way though.

History is full of change that did not come easy. The world is scarred by the pain of progress desperately pushing its way through fear and prejudice held by those that had such a comfortable position in the world of old that they saw no need for it to alter in any way.

I was just a child when I heard the word "pandemic" for the first time. I remember the daily body count. I remember the debates amidst the dying. But mostly I remember the masks... and how they signaled a new world people were afraid to embrace even as it sought to secure them.

As we looked at the plans for construction provided by the worker bees, I could see in the eyes of many that they looked at the domes as masks, not protection.

Perhaps the only reason the people of the town ultimately acquiesced was due to the fact that as the Winderbergs foretold, the temperature began dropping a degree a day with no end in sight.

Welcome to the new world.

CHAPTER 10

This House Is Not a Home

The construction of the domes and aboveground tunnels that would connect them was no easy task, but the workers bees made it seem so.

Without pause, rest and or complaint they unloaded materials directed us where to place and how to assist.

These domes were not going to be homes... they were not going to resemble them nor possess any comforts afforded by a house that benefitted from the years of items both practical and personal the families that lived in them placed there.

They were domes.

The contents of each would not be similar, it would be the same. There was no design or specifications specific to the individual personalities of the inhabitants.

The domes would hold beds and little else. There would be no electricity only solar. Food would be stored in a common area as would most other items that were deemed sharable. As one would imagine, this created issues as well.

It's strange how sometimes when situations push people together, they immediately bond and how other times regardless of the circumstances... or perhaps because of... it pulls neighbors and even families apart.

It was the strength and mutual respect given Deputy Pete by the townspeople that kept a tenuous peace amongst them.

Tenuous and temporary.

Chapter 11

The Tenuous and the Temporary

Every town and or city has their fair share of Agneses and Tarbers. What every city does not have is enough Deputy Petes.

There is always that person, when building a bridge, that screams, 'You're building it in the wrong direction,' even though there's only one direction it can be built to be effective and or purposeful. That's the thing about direction… it may be right but not everyone wants to go right, everyone just wants to be right.

Now, there is nothing wrong with wanting to be right, but when you try and force what you think is right into a box that it will not fit in because it is wrong, because you are wrong, you end up not bending the box but destroying it. The box, the building, the country.

As we built the domes to protect what was ours, our lives, as the temperature continued to drop with no variance but to drop, we watched as parts of the world panicked.

Temperatures were dropping steadily everywhere. Now where some regions would not necessarily look upon this with alarm, those areas that were never visited by cold, and certainly foreign to freeze were unsettled by the lack of answers as to why.

If it's possible to be wrong with the answer right before you, imagine the possibilities of wrong assumptions when what is right has yet to reveal itself. Imagine the chaos. Envision the fear.

The world seemed to be falling apart, in slow motion, one degree at a time while the degree of behavior from man to man was declining at a far more rapid rate.

I asked Mr. Winderberg why he did not tell the world what was coming... why he chose one small town, one pocket to protect... there was a long pause... and then he exhaled and simply said...

"Not everyone can be saved."

He explained how the seasons themselves are surrounded by death. There is the death of the season before and the death of the season that replaced it when it too, is time for another season.

I looked at it as the leaves on a tree. When fall arrives, the leaves die. But not every leaf falls at the same time, and some don't fall at all. The tree seems to know which ones to let go.

He added that sometimes you have to prove there is a reason to be saved before some will allow you to save them. We would be that proof.

Chapter 12

Elemental

We enter the domes. There is no fanfare there is no fear, there is just acceptance. Where at the beginning we first wondered if these protective enclosures would be needed or if it was just some fantastical folly, by the end, as this clear dome was finishing its construction just outside the town it was temporarily to replace, the elements made us believers.

It was cold. Bitterly cold. The kind of cold that makes you forget what warmth felt like. Not the kind of cold that makes you reach out for warmth, for how can you reach out for what you can't remember... But the kind of cold that forces you to accept that you will never be anything but a cousin to ice.

Protective clothing provided by the worker bees as was most everything else during construction kept us alive while we were outside. But there came a point in time where we were forced inside the incomplete dome, watching as other domes arose and were finished around us. Those of us that chose to enter.

Seven people decided to go against the majority. Seven people that determined their ideology was more important than fact. The fact that the temperature was dropping with no end in sight, only ice.

Coincidentally, the seven all belonged to the same family. The family of Agnus.

I wonder how after seeing the cold and ice... after witnessing everything freeze over... how after looking into the otherworldly eyes of the Winderbergs, she still was able to wrap herself in doubt.

I wonder how long it was before she realized she was wrong and how long it was after she realized it was too late.

I wonder if the other six members of her family had to realize they were wrong or never had a choice to be right because the decision was not their own.

I mostly wonder this when I'm looking outside at their frozen bodies a few yards away from the doors that were closed and then entry became impossible.

Chapter 13

2050

(pt. 2)

"I'll be brave for both of us," I have just told Deputy Pete after we both have rappelled down beneath the ground.

We are no longer secure within the sanctuary provided by the domes, but we had to leave the security to maintain the security. Something went wrong. And it not only threatened the survival of everyone inside, but the survival of those that came to save us.

"That's good," Deputy Pete says. "Because I'm pretty scared."

He winks as if joking, but I know he's not. I also know now is not the time to be truthful and let him know that I'm pretty afraid myself. Somehow, I feel he knows as the time spent in the domes drew us unexpectedly closer together.

It has been approximately four months since the doors to the interconnected domes were closed shut. The temperature finally stabilized to where it was no longer dropping. But that didn't matter. The temperature stabilized at the degree of death. To even step outside meant instantaneous freezing.

To make matters worse, if that were even possible, we were cut off from the outside world. There was no television, no radio, no internet, in effect, there was no outside world. It felt like behind us, the world that once existed was dead and in front of us, the world we could see through the clear walls of the dome was death.

You can understand how that might drive people insane. How one's grasp of reality might be adversely affected and how they would look to whomever they thought provided the most strength.

Inexplicably that was me. I was their voice from the beginning and that, unlike the seasons, never changed. For me... That person was Deputy Pete... his voice was my strength because he believed in my voice.

We were beneath the Earth because of the situation above.

The domes were doing their job of protecting and sustaining fantastically. The worker bees, who were no longer with us... having somehow, somewhere, simply vanished, had planned and constructed the domes flawlessly for our needs. There was never any worry that they would crack beneath the extreme cold even as we observed things outside do that very thing.

But nothing goes wrong until something goes wrong and often by the time you notice something has gone wrong, it has progressed into something that is now, dangerously wrong.

Water.

Life needs water. Water grows life, maintains it and sustains it. And one day... it was simply gone. The specialized piping system constructed to keep the water flowing through it seemingly dried up. This was impossible though as the source of water was endless. It just somehow stopped.

There was enough water stored to sustain us for at least a month. But eventually we would need more so the problem could not simply be ignored. But... and when something goes wrong, there is often a 'but' that will make it exponentially worse, but the Winderbergs were not doing well.

Since I'd known the Winderbergs, though older, they exuded a vibrance, an energy, an aura that made them appear to be the youngest, healthiest people in any given room.

But the stoppage of water through the piping system troubled them. And I had yet to see them troubled so now I was as well.

I noticed that from the moment they discovered the issues with the pipes they immediately stopped drinking from our secondary sources. Now being a nurse, I know how long the body can be deprived of water before it affects the outward appearance. It may vary from person to person, but it is never immediate as it was with the Winderbergs.

Whatever they were, wherever they were from, and I wasn't too sure of either, they needed water and they needed it now.

When I asked why they would not drink from

our backup supply that is when they were forced to answer at least some of the questions I had about them I never had the courage to ask.

"The amount of water we need to live would prevent you from doing the same." He said.

I asked why and he told me, that origin of their essence required almost ten times the amount of water we needed to survive and that if they were to drink from our month's supply of water it would be gone in a matter of days.

I looked into both their eyes and mine welled up with the water they so desperately needed.

Here they were, people, beings that had come to save us... sacrificing themselves selflessly so they could save us again.

The freeze itself, Mr. Winderberg had predicted would be done soon. So, there was little urgency for us to discover the issue with the pipes. If the

Winderbergs were right, and they had yet to be wrong, we wouldn't need the piping system before we would need the piping system. But they did. They needed it yesterday and here we were already on today. It would have been easy to just watch them die. But I'm a nurse... and for me... it's never easy to watch someone die. Even if their death saves lives.

CHAPTER 14

The Root of It All

Even though the piping was primarily above ground, it did have to reach beneath for its source. So underground we would have to go. But that meant first we would have to venture outside and how were we to do that when there was nothing outside but white, icy death.

The Winderbergs were vague as to how and

what we could do to save their lives. It was almost as if they didn't want to be saved, or that they were so concerned about me that they didn't want me risking my own survival for theirs. But how could that be. They barely knew me.

It was actually Deputy Pete that reminded me of what this was all about. The change of seasons. The elements. The crystals.

I had been given four crystals by The Winderbergs early on. I used one to bring a "winter" to a sky of fire thus extinguishing it and saving us from becoming ash.

Perhaps... Perhaps the remaining three crystals represented the remaining three seasons.

If winter had saved us from heat, then summer would be our savior from the cold. And that is how Deputy Pete and I found ourselves below ground.

We could not open the doors to the dome to exit as this could result not only in our immediate deaths but the deaths of all inside. What we could do was use one of the access doors from the floor that had been constructed to reach critical equipment that would not withstand the freeze above. Make no mistake, it was cold below, too cold for anything to survive but not so cold that everything would crack.

Before we opened the doors, we put on two protective thermal suits left by the worker bees. We cleared everyone form the dome section containing the floor access door, for fear the moments it would open would be too dangerous. This would prove almost as equally as difficult as the task before us due to those that had no problem letting the Winderbergs die but were not willing to risk my, or especially their demise… which some tied into my own.

I was not going to be deterred from my mission and this they knew. So, they all retreated to other units and sections of the dome town.

Deputy Pete and I stood above the door. Before he leaned down to unlatch the lock we just stood there and looked into each other's eyes even though both our faces were shielded.

"You don't need to go with me," I told him. "I can do this alone."

He looked at me for a moment then responded, "And let you hog all the glory."

I laughed... And as difficult as it was, I could see him smiling through the suit.

I said, "No, really..."

And he added, "Really... I want to." And then without saying another word he leaned down, unlatched the door and slowly pulled it open as I held his hand with one of mine and with the other, I clutched the crystal that began to glow, surrounding us in a warmth that blocked the cold from piercing through our souls.

Once we were down below, we were both surprised by what we saw, by what we never knew existed... It was as if beneath us a complete world, sustaining ours was in place.

Our feet were on solid ground, even though above our heads was a roof of solid ground. Before us pathways lined with branches that as we walked and I observed them more closely, revealed themselves to be roots. We were walking through the entire root system of every tree above us, and it was amazing.

Neither Deputy Pete nor I knew what we were looking for. But I decided we should walk... just walk... until we saw something that didn't look right. And that was going to be difficult when everything that surrounded us looked like nothing we'd ever seen before.

Occasionally, the path would be difficult to walk as roots would entangle us or simply obscure the direction we wanted to take. But in an odd way, this helped. Nothing up until this point had been easy so I felt the only right way was going to be the hard way.

Even more odd... the more we walked the more familiar the unfamiliar became.

"I feel like I've seen this before," I say to Deputy Pete.

"Seen what?" he asks. "Roots?"

"No... I say... this pathway... this landscape... this way... I feel like I've seen it. Walked it."

"That's impossible."

I turn and look at him. Is he really calling something impossible as we find ourselves in an impossible situation? I think that he senses my incredulous smirk.

"Yeah… You're right," he smartly adds.

And then it hits me. I look to the right… Then I look to my left. I look behind me then I turn back and look straight ahead.

"I know where we are," I say.

"Where are we?"

"Home."

That's why it looked all so familiar to me. I can tell by the cluster of roots and their placements that I am on my grandfather's farm. My farm.

It all becomes clear to me. I know why I was chosen. I know why I am here. And more importantly I know where we must go.

"Follow me," I say, and he does.

I quicken the pace now that I am familiar with the road. I remember the faces of the Winderbergs and how sullen and lifeless they were. There is no time to stroll.

And there it is... straight ahead, the roots of the mighty tree where my grandparents met beneath. Right where they should be. As massive and sprawling as I would imagine them to be.

How do I know it's the tree? Because, like the Winderbergs, the roots are gray and dying.

"Is it dead?" Deputy Pete asks.

"No," I say, hoping I am right. "But it will be soon."

"What should we do?"

"I don't know, Pete." I say. "What do you think?"

We both stand there in silence... Until it is broken by Deputy Pete.

"It's been a long winter. Too long…" he says. "It's needs spring."

"How do I give it spring?" I ask.

"Easy." He says. "It's in your hand, Sunflower." I smile.

He's right… I look down and open my clutched palm. Inside two crystals remain. I have used both summer and winter. One has to be spring.

I choose the one with a yellowish hue. It reminds me of a sunflower.

I hold it out and everything around us glows yellow and the roots slowly pull all the yellow from around us into them as if drinking water from a spring.

We watch as the roots slowly seem to strengthen, slowly seem to regain life.

"What do you think happened?" Deputy Pete asks. "Why do you think it began to die?"

I don't know that I have an answer. So, I stand there for a moment trying to come up with one.

I keep remembering the stories my grandparents told me as a child. I remember not only the closeness the tree held for them but for me as well.

I think about all that is happening around us. I think of all that has happened around the world. You cannot think about the world without thinking about nature. And now I think about all the ways man has betrayed nature… stolen from it… changed it… erased it… ignored it…

And yet for centuries nature continued to sustain us. Repair itself and feed us. Sometimes doing both simultaneously.

How exhausting must that be? How long can one system maintain that degree of hurt and continue to help?

How long?

"I think the tree finally had enough. It had no more   life left to give… And…"

I pause.

"And what?" Deputy Pete asks.

"And the leaves gave us one last chance.

CHAPTER 15

The Life of Leaves

It has been four months since I emerged from beneath ground to the hope that spring brings. That is not to say that all is back to normal but the hope that it can and will now springs eternal.

We are still in the domes... The world doesn't freeze overnight, and the process of unfreezing takes even more time. Especially if you want to minimize the damage wrought by the cold.

There are little signs of life that we witness through the glass of the domes... but so little... so fragile... we dare not disturb the process with our presence. In that respect... I think we have learned.

The question will be, for how long? And who? Are there more survivors than we? Are there people who knew what was coming, and prepared in the way the Winderbergs had us prepare, on their own?

What will the world be when we venture out for the first time? Will television be there to show us? Will the internet be up to connect us? Should any of this happen? Or would it just set us back on the road our arrogance shook us from like an earthquake destroying a bridge and removing the road before us?

The Winderbergs, before they left, explained to me the life of trees and how the leaves themselves are children of nature.

Everything you want to know about life he said,

can be seen in the evolution of a leaf.

Perhaps that is because the souls of those that benefitted by nature are deposited back into nature. Perhaps karma is that you become what you took advantage of ,and therefore have to teach those after you not to.

Or perhaps the leaves, the petals, the blades of grass are a higher form of life that become us in order to help us... or more importantly protect themselves.

That would mean the mysterious disease that took my grandparents was nature's way of protecting itself. At least that's what I thought until the Winderbergs spoke to me.

They explained it was a little bit of everything I wondered about and some things I could never comprehend.

They explained sometimes disease calls a form back to where it will serve a greater purpose. And sometimes parents disappear but never leave you, in fact, are now able to protect you in ways they couldn't otherwise.

They would not explain exactly where my parents were, but said, that their importance was no less simply because I did not see them. In that way they said, so too was the importance of nature.

www.ingramcontent.com/pod-product-compliance
Lightning Source LLC
Chambersburg PA
CBHW071142250626
47159CB00006B/2261